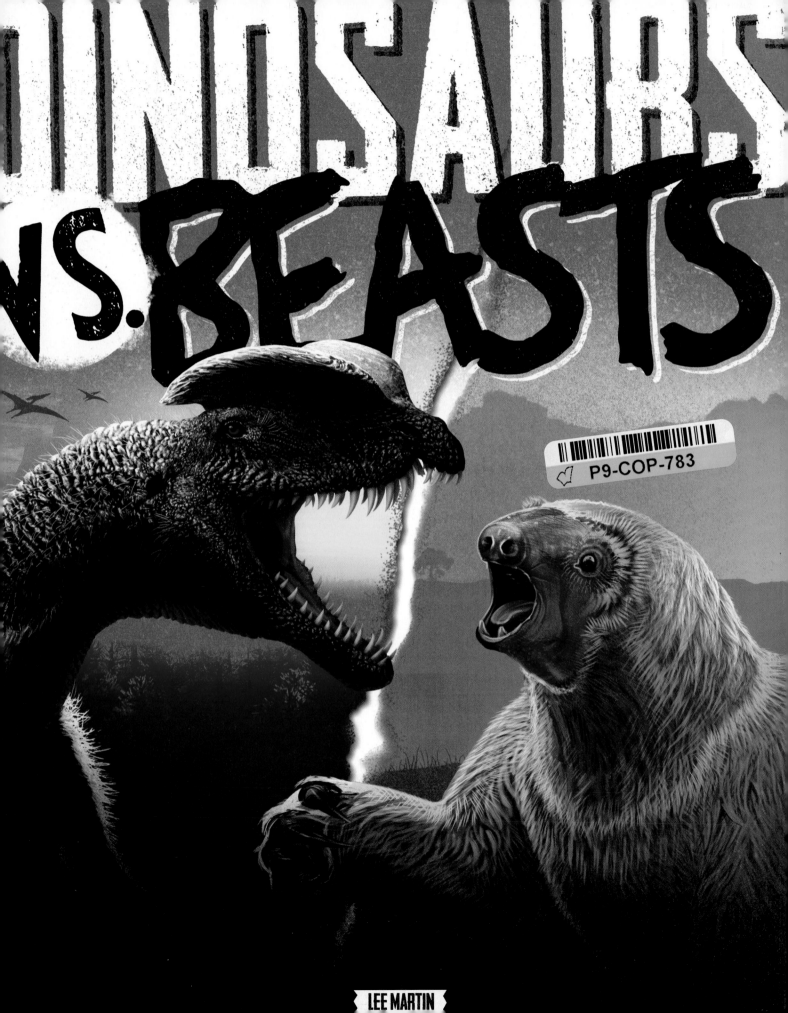

DINOSAURS VS. BEASTS

LEE MARTIN

This edition published by Scholastic Inc., 557 Broadway, New York, NY 10012, by arrangement with becker&mayer! LLC. Scholastic and associated logos are trademarks and/or registered trademarks of Scholastic Inc.

Scholastic Inc., New York, NY

becker&mayer!
BOOK PRODUCERS
Produced by becker&mayer!, LLC
11120 NE 33rd Place, Suite 101
Bellevue, WA 98004
www.beckermayer.com

Author: Lee Martin
Designer: Sam Dawson
Illustrators: RJ Palmer and Alex Ries
Editor: Leah Jenness
Photo researcher: Farley Bookout
Production coordinator: Tom Miller

ISBN: 978-0-545-93161-8

CONTENTS

DINOSAUR VS. BEAST

SETTING THE STAGE

Dinosaurs and prehistoric beasts were some of the largest, fiercest, and wildest-looking creatures to ever roam the Earth. In this epic showdown, creatures from different eras— yet uniquely adapted to their own time—go head-to-head. Let's learn more about where and when these combatants lived.

THE AGE OF REPTILES

When we talk about dinosaurs, we're referring to a certain kind of creature that lived on land during the Mesozoic Era, often called the Age of Reptiles. (Sea creatures—such as the Liopleurodon—and creatures that flew—such as Quetzalcoatlus, a pterosaur—were not dinosaurs.)

Scientists don't know for sure what dinosaurs looked like, or what sounds they made, or how they behaved. Paleontologists study the fossil remains. Then they use the anatomy and behavior of modern animals to inform their understanding of how dinosaurs stood, walked, hunted, ate, and interacted.

MESOZOIC ERA

The Mesozoic Era is divided into three time periods: Triassic, Jurassic, and Cretaceous. At the beginning of the Mesozoic Era, the continents on Earth were all jammed together into one big mass called Pangaea. The Earth was much warmer then than it is today.

TRIASSIC	JURASSIC	CRETACEOUS
250–200 million years ago (MYA)	200–145 MYA	145–65 MYA
During the Triassic period, most of the dinosaurs were carnivores (meat-eaters) and preyed on each other. The land was covered with huge seed plants—ferns and palm- and tree-like plants.	During the Jurassic period, the sea levels were much higher than they are now. The climate in the middle of Pangaea was hot and dry. But as the land mass began to break apart, water flooded in. Plants and trees in temperate and subtropical forests grew plentifully. Mammals evolved, but were still small in size. Dinosaurs had a lot to eat and thrived during this time.	During the Cretaceous period, dinosaurs reached their peak in size. Also, mammals flourished and the first flowers appeared. The flowering plants quickly overtook the primitive plants that had been growing on Earth, forever altering the environment.

About 65 million years ago, the Cretaceous period ended with a mass extinction of the dinosaurs, bringing an end to the Age of Reptiles and a beginning to the Age of Mammals.

THE LAST ICE AGE

About 60 million years after the end of the Cretaceous period, the Pleistocene Epoch began. Often known as the last Ice Age, it lasted until about 11,700 years ago.

At this time, the continents had moved to the positions they are in now. The sea levels were lower, and the Earth was much colder. Glaciers and ice sheets covered huge areas of Earth. These glaciers radically changed the face of the continents. Their movement over time formed lakes, changed rivers' paths, and left huge deposits of sand and gravel in their wakes.

MESOZOIC ERA

MODERN WORLD

The first *Homo sapiens*—humans—evolved during the Pleistocene, and this was the age of the giant mammals, or megafauna such as Woolly Mammoths, Smilodons, and Giant Sloths. Most of these animals were covered with thick fur to help protect them from the cold. Birds and crocodiles also flourished. In many areas, there wasn't a lot of vegetation, but the plants that grew were similar to the plants we have today, including grasses, conifers such as pine trees, and broadleaf deciduous trees such as oaks and beeches.

There's a lot of debate about what caused the extinction of the giant mammals. Most believe it was a combination of climate change and possibly overhunting by humans.

LET THE BATTLE BEGIN!

NOW IT'S TIME TO PIT THESE CREATURES FROM TWO VERY DIFFERENT WORLDS AGAINST EACH OTHER.

WHO WILL REIGN? DINO OR BEAST?

MAY THE BEST-ADAPTED CREATURE WIN!

T. REX VS. WOOLLY MAMMOTH

HEIGHT: 20 feet (6 m)
WEIGHT: 14,000 pounds (6,350 kg)
DIET: Carnivore
KNOWN PREY: Hadrosaur, Triceratops, Edmontosaurus
FOSSILS FOUND: North America
LIVED: Late Cretaceous

SPEED:	STRENGTH:	BRAINS:	ATTACK:	DEFENSE:
7	9	10	10	5

LIZARD KING

T. rex had sharp teeth for hooking into opponents' flesh, and claws built for ripping and gripping. Keen eyesight and hearing also made it one of the fiercest prehistoric predators.

THE SHOWDOWN

Two famous prehistoric animals go head-to-head in a match that pits tooth against hoof. The Tyrannosaurus rex is bigger, with a ferocious bite, but how will it fare against the Woolly Mammoth's large, fearsome tusks?

HEIGHT TO SHOULDER: 10 feet (3 m)
WEIGHT: 12,000 pounds (5,440 kg)
DIET: Herbivore
KNOWN PREDATORS: Saber-toothed cat, early humans
FOSSILS FOUND: All over the Northern Hemisphere
LIVED: Pleistocene

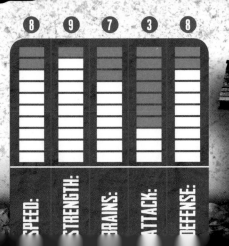

8 9 7 3 8

SPEED: STRENGTH: BRAINS: ATTACK: DEFENSE:

WOOLLY WONDER

The Woolly Mammoth was bulky and built for defense. Its 18-foot (5.5-m) tusks each weighed up to 150 pounds (68 kg), and packed a mighty punch in a fight with any predator.

VELOCIRAPTOR VS. GIANT SLOTH
(Megatherium)

HEIGHT: 3 feet (0.9 m)
WEIGHT: 45–65 pounds (20–30 kg)
DIET: Carnivore
KNOWN PREY: Reptiles, amphibians, smaller dinosaurs
FOSSILS FOUND: Asia: Mongolia and China
LIVED: Late Cretaceous

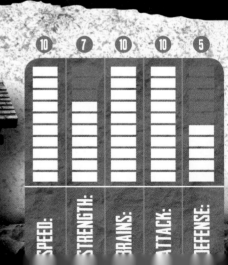

10	7	10	10	5
SPEED:	STRENGTH:	BRAINS:	ATTACK:	DEFENSE:

BRAINY
With its big brain, Velociraptor was a smart and speedy hunter. Each foot had a large claw shaped like a sickle, which it used to hold on to and rip into its prey. Its long tail gave it balance and stability when running and turning at high speeds.

THE SHOWDOWN

The slow-moving but massive Giant Sloth faces the quick and clever Velociraptor. Although small, the Velociraptor has sharp, serrated teeth and fearsome back talons. But will it be able to avoid the sloth's giant claws?

HEIGHT: 19.5 feet (6 m)
WEIGHT: 4 tons
DIET: Herbivore
KNOWN PREDATORS: Humans
FOSSILS FOUND: Southeastern North America, Mexico, Central America
LIVED: Pleistocene

BRAWNY

Sluggish but huge, the Giant Sloth was not a creature to tangle with. It had three huge claws on each paw, which it probably used to dig for food, as well as powerful limbs that could deliver a strong swipe. For defense, it had small bones embedded in its skin under its long, coarse fur that acted like body armor.

2 8 5 2 8

SPEED: STRENGTH: BRAINS: ATTACK: DEFENSE:

SPINOSAURUS VS. GLYPTODONT

HEIGHT TO SHOULDER: 14 feet (4.3 m)
WEIGHT: 6 tons or more
DIET: Carnivore
KNOWN PREY: Fish
FOSSILS FOUND: Africa
LIVED: Mid-Cretaceous

SPINY LIZARD

Spinosaurus was huge—bigger even than T. rex. Its sharp teeth were set in crocodile-like jaws, perfect for snaring fish. It likely patrolled the edges of waterways for prey. The long spines that grew from its backbone were covered with skin, forming a crest or sail.

6   8   8   10   6

SPEED: STRENGTH: BRAINS: ATTACK: DEFENSE:

THE SHOWDOWN

A huge dinosaur battles the tough Glyptodont. Spinosaurus has an intimidating crest and a mouthful of sharp teeth. But the Glyptodont is heavily armored: The Spinosaurus had better watch out for that tail. The Glyptodont could break its legs with it.

SIZING THEM UP!

LENGTH	LENGTH
40 feet (12 m)	9.8 feet (3 m)

HEIGHT: Shell height, 4.9 feet (1.5 m)

WEIGHT: 1 ton or more

DIET: Herbivore

KNOWN PREDATOR: Saber-toothed cat

FOSSILS FOUND: Southern United States and Mexico

LIVED: Pleistocene

2   6   3   -   2   -   10

SPEED: STRENGTH: BRAINS: ATTACK: DEFENSE:

ANCIENT ARMADILLO

This massive, tank-like creature was a relative of the armadillo. Its dome-shaped shell, made up of about 2,000 interlocking plates, offered protection from predators. Its head, too, was shielded with a cap of bony plates. It used its mighty tail to wallop would-be trespassers.

COELOPHYSIS VS. DIRE WOLF
(Canis dirus)

HEIGHT TO SHOULDER: 3 feet (0.9 m)
WEIGHT: 100 pounds (45.3 kg)
DIET: Carnivore
KNOWN PREY: Reptiles, small mammals
FOSSILS FOUND: North America, Southern Africa, China
LIVED: Late Triassic to Early Jurassic

SPEED DEMON

Coelophysis was built for speed. Its leg bones were almost hollow, which made it light and able to run fast. It seized its prey with long front limbs and held it with claw-tipped fingers. Strong hind legs suggest it was an agile hunter.

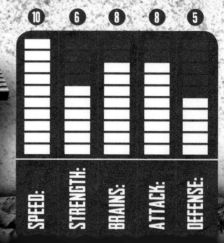

SPEED:	STRENGTH:	BRAINS:	ATTACK:	DEFENSE:
10	6	8	8	5

THE SHOWDOWN

Two clever creatures face off. The Coelophysis is small and light, but very fast. The Dire Wolf is strong and smart. Who will outwit the other? Will the Coelophysis be able to grab the Dire Wolf with its claws? Or will the Dire Wolf use its strength and bite to take down the dinosaur?

SIZING THEM UP!

LENGTH	LENGTH
8–10 feet (2.4–3 m)	About 5 feet (1.5 m)

HEIGHT AT SHOULDER: 2.6 feet (80 cm)
WEIGHT: 115 pounds (53 kg)
DIET: Carnivore
KNOWN PREY: Horses, bison
FOSSILS FOUND: North America, Central America, western South America
LIVED: Pleistocene

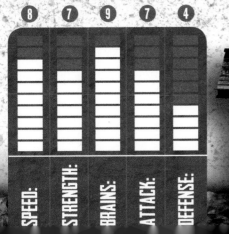

8	7	9	7	4
SPEED:	STRENGTH:	BRAINS:	ATTACK:	DEFENSE:

FEARSOME DOG

A Dire Wolf was only slightly larger than a modern-day wolf. But it was broader and more heavily muscled, and its bite was much more forceful. Like modern wolves, it most likely hunted in packs and debilitated its prey with a series of shallow, painful bites.

15

HERRERASAURUS VS. MEGALOCEROS
(Giant Deer)

HEIGHT TO SHOULDER: 4 feet (1.2 m)
WEIGHT: 460 pounds (210 kg)
DIET: Carnivore
KNOWN PREY: Small reptiles, smaller dinosaurs
FOSSILS FOUND: South America, Argentina
LIVED: Middle to Late Triassic

10	8	7	10	8
SPEED:	STRENGTH:	BRAINS:	ATTACK:	DEFENSE:

FIERCE BITER

Because it was so fast and nimble, the Herrerasaurus tackled prey much larger than itself. Once it was able to snatch its prey with its inward-curving teeth, there was no getting away.

THE SHOWDOWN

Megaloceros has the advantage of size. But while the Herrerasaurus isn't huge, it definitely isn't tiny, either. And the minute it gets its teeth on the Megaloceros's flank, you can bet it won't let go. But will the Megaloceros's strong hooves and enormous antlers keep its opponent at bay?

SIZING THEM UP!

LENGTH 13 feet (3.9 m)	LENGTH 8 feet (2.5 m)

HEIGHT: 6.8 feet (2.1 m)
WEIGHT: 1,100 pounds (500 kg)
DIET: Herbivore
KNOWN PREDATORS: Wolves, humans
FOSSILS FOUND: Europe, northern Asia, Africa
LIVED: Pleistocene

6 6 6 6 7

SPEED:
STRENGTH:
BRAINS:
ATTACK:
DEFENSE:

ENORMOUSLY ANTLERED

The largest deer in the history of the world used its antlers—a rack that measured up to 12 feet (3.65 m) tip to tip—as defense against would-be predators. The female also boxed with its powerful front hooves.

PACHYCEPHALOSAURUS VS. WOODLAND MUSKOX

HEIGHT TO SHOULDER: 6 feet (1.8 m)
WEIGHT: 990 pounds (450 kg)
DIET: Mostly herbivore
KNOWN PREDATOR: Tyrannosaurus Rex
FOSSILS FOUND: North America
LIVED: Late Cretaceous

BONE HEAD

Pachycephalosaurus was called a "boneheaded" dinosaur thanks to the top of its skull, which was 20 times thicker than those of other dinosaurs its size. Scientists think it may have used its massive head to slam into enemies as a last-ditch defensive effort.

SPEED:	STRENGTH:	BRAINS:	ATTACK:	DEFENSE:
7	6	4	5	5

THE SHOWDOWN

This is a match between two hardheaded creatures. The Pachycephalosaurus has an incredibly thick skull, but it isn't as durable as the Woodland Muskox's horns. While the Muskox has a thick coat of fur, it may not be able to withstand the Pachy's attack.

HEIGHT AT SHOULDER: 3–5 feet (0.9–1.5 m)
WEIGHT: 900 pounds (408 kg)
DIET: Herbivore
KNOWN PREDATORS: Giant Short-Faced Bear
FOSSILS FOUND: Siberia, North America
LIVED: Pleistocene

4   7   4   6   6

SPEED: STRENGTH: BRAINS: ATTACK: DEFENSE:

HARD HORNS

The Woodland Muskox also had a hard head and a massive set of horns, which it used to ram rival oxen. Its squat, heavy body was covered with a coat of long, thick hair, offering protection from the cold—and perhaps a predator's teeth and claws.

TRICERATOPS VS. MASTODON

HEIGHT TO SHOULDER: 15 feet (4.6 m)
WEIGHT: Up to 10 tons
DIET: Herbivore
KNOWN PREDATOR: Tyrannosaurus rex
FOSSILS FOUND: North America
LIVED: Late Cretaceous

THREE-HORNED TANK

Triceratops had three horns—two sharp 3-foot (98-cm) horns on its brow and another on its snout. Its strong neck frill was made of solid bone, and could offer protection. Plus, it was built like a tank.

SPEED:	STRENGTH:	BRAINS:	ATTACK:	DEFENSE:
3	7	3	5	8

THE SHOWDOWN

At five tons, the Mastodon weighs only half as much as the Triceratops. The Triceratops has three amazing horns and a neck frill. But the Mastodon has its own set of terrifying tusks, and is perhaps a bit more crafty.

SIZING THEM UP!

LENGTH	LENGTH
30 feet (9 m)	48 feet (14.8 m)

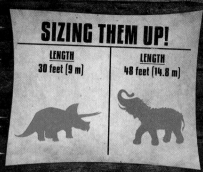

HEIGHT: 8 feet (2.4 m)
WEIGHT: 5 tons
DIET: Herbivore
KNOWN PREDATORS: Humans
FOSSILS FOUND: Asia, Africa, Europe, North America, Central America
LIVED: Pleistocene

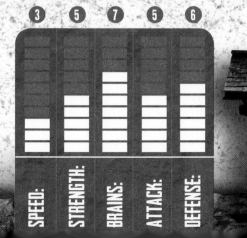

3 5 7 5 6

SPEED: STRENGTH: BRAINS: ATTACK: DEFENSE:

TERRIFYING TUSKS

The Mastodon's spear-like tusks grew up to 8.2 feet (2.5 m) long. Their footprints have been measured at up to 1.6 feet (50 cm) across. Its eyesight was poor, however, so it could become aggressive quickly if surprised.

21

ANKYLOSAURUS VS. WOOLLY RHINO
(Coelodonta)

HEIGHT TO SHOULDER: 4 feet (1.2 m)
WEIGHT: 4 tons
DIET: Herbivore
KNOWN PREDATOR: Tyrannosaurus rex
FOSSILS FOUND: Asia, North America
LIVED: Late Cretaceous

ARMORED BUS

Built like an armored bus, the Ankylosaurus had bony spikes covering its back and tail. It had a heavy club of bone at the end of its tail, too. When swung from side to side, it could kill an attacking predator.

3	6	2	4	10

SPEED: 3
STRENGTH: 6
BRAINS: 2
ATTACK: 4
DEFENSE: 10

THE SHOWDOWN

This matchup pits hulk against hulk. The Ankylosaurus is protected by its spikes and plates, while the Woolly Rhino has a thick coat of fur. The Woolly Rhino could charge the awkward-moving Ankylosaurus, but the dino could debilitate it with a swing of its club-like tail.

SIZING THEM UP!

LENGTH 25–35 feet (7.5–10.7 m)	LENGTH 11.5 feet (3.5 m)

HEIGHT AT SHOULDER: 6 feet (2 m)
WEIGHT: 3 tons
DIET: Herbivore
KNOWN PREDATORS: Humans
FOSSILS FOUND: Asia, Europe
LIVED: Pleistocene

3 5 3 4 6

SPEED: STRENGTH: BRAINS: ATTACK: DEFENSE:

FIERCE HORNS

The Woolly Rhino was a grass-eater, but predators would have to watch out for its two horns. The front one was 3 feet (1 m) long and very sharp, and the other was 2 feet (60 cm) long. They were particularly deadly when the Rhino would charge.

GIGANOTOSAURUS VS. GIANT SHORT-FACED BEAR
(Arctodus simus)

HEIGHT TO HEAD: 23 feet (7 m)
WEIGHT: Up to 10 tons
DIET: Carnivore
KNOWN PREY: Large herbivore dinosaurs
FOSSILS FOUND: South America
LIVED: Late Cretaceous

THE GIANT
Giganotosaurus was one of the biggest meat-eaters ever. Its skull was 6 feet (1.8 m) long, and it had a mouthful of sizable 8-inch (20.3-cm) teeth. Its brain, though, was only about the size of a banana.

5	10	2	10	6
SPEED:	STRENGTH:	BRAINS:	ATTACK:	DEFENSE:

THE SHOWDOWN

Okay. The Giganotosaurus is huge. There's just no getting around that. But the Giant Short-Faced Bear is faster, and at 1,500 pounds, it's no lightweight. Will it be able to evade the teeth and claws of the Giganotosaurus and use its own sharp teeth and claws to take out the giant dino?

SIZING THEM UP!

LENGTH 43 feet (13 m)	LENGTH 12 feet (3.6 m)

HEIGHT TO SHOULDER: 5.5 feet (1.7 m)
WEIGHT: 2,200 pounds (997 kg)
DIET: Carnivore or omnivore
KNOWN PREY: Perhaps horses; perhaps a scavenger
FOSSILS FOUND: North America
LIVED: Pleistocene

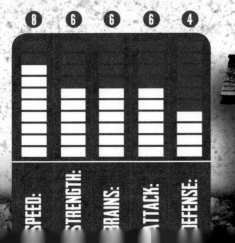

8	6	6	6	4
SPEED:	STRENGTH:	BRAINS:	ATTACK:	DEFENSE:

COOL DUDE

Not only does it have a cool name, but the Giant Short-faced Bear was a large and fast predator. Its long legs allowed it to cover a lot of territory and take on big prey. Some scientists think it could run up to 40 miles (64 km) per hour.

DEINONYCHUS VS. GIANT BEAVER
(Castoroides)

HEIGHT: 5 feet (1.5 m)
WEIGHT: 175 pounds (80 kg)
DIET: Carnivore
KNOWN PREY: Anything it wanted to catch
FOSSILS FOUND: Western North America
LIVED: Mid-Cretaceous

10	5	9	10	5

THE HUNTER

Deinonychus had wide hands tipped with claws for grasping at prey. Even more intimidating was the large, curved claw on the second toe of each foot—measuring about 4–5 inches (10–13 cm). Additionally, it was also smart and fast—in other words, a super-deadly predator.

SPEED: STRENGTH: BRAINS: ATTACK: DEFENSE:

THE SHOWDOWN

It's humongous rodent against a master hunter. Deinonychus is fast, smart, and deadly. The Giant Beaver is heavier and stronger. Deinonychus has terrifying claws, but it will have to beware of the Beaver's outsized teeth.

HEIGHT: 3.2 feet (1 m)
WEIGHT: Up to 220 pounds (100 kg)
DIET: Herbivore
KNOWN PREDATORS: Large Ice Age predators
FOSSILS FOUND: North America
LIVED: Pleistocene

6 6 4 4 6

SPEED: STRENGTH: BRAINS: ATTACK: DEFENSE:

REMARKABLE RODENT

The largest rodent to live in North America, the Giant Beaver had teeth that grew up to 6 inches long (15 cm). It was heavy, too, with stout limbs to support its weight. It's a solid competitor.

STEGOSAURUS VS. CAVE BEAR
(Ursus spelaeus)

HEIGHT AT HIPS: About 9 feet (2.7 m)
WEIGHT: 6,800 pounds (3,100 kg)
DIET: Herbivore
KNOWN PREDATOR: Allosaurus
FOSSILS FOUND: Asia, North America
LIVED: Late Jurassic

SPIKED TAIL

The Stegosaurus had huge, flat plates that ran down its back and a tail tipped with four big spikes. Obviously, it was able to defend itself, but it may have been hampered by a brain the size of a walnut.

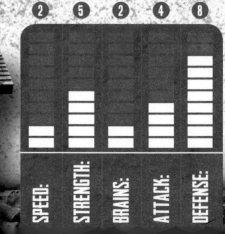

2	5	2	4	8
SPEED:	STRENGTH:	BRAINS:	ATTACK:	DEFENSE:

THE SHOWDOWN

When the Stegosaurus and the Cave Bear clash, the Stegosaurus's bony plates will offer protection, and it may be able to do some damage with its spike-tipped tail. But its serious disadvantage is its lack of brainpower. Perhaps what the Cave Bear lacks in armor, it can make up for with smarts and strong teeth and claws.

SIZING THEM UP!

LENGTH 30 feet (9 m)	LENGTH 9.8 feet (3 m)

HEIGHT, STANDING: 9 feet (3 m)
WEIGHT: Up to 1,322 pounds (600 kg)
DIET: Herbivore, omnivore
KNOWN PREDATORS: Humans
FOSSILS FOUND: European and Russian mountains
LIVED: Pleistocene

7 5 6 6 5

SPEED: STRENGTH: BRAINS: ATTACK: DEFENSE:

BIG BAD BEAR

The Cave Bear, an ancestor of the modern brown bear, had short, powerful legs that supported its heavy body. Although it was an herbivore, it surely would have used its large claws and canines against any creature that disturbed it.

DILOPHOSAURUS VS. EUSMILUS

HEIGHT TO SHOULDER: 7 feet (2.1 m)
WEIGHT: 650–1,000 pounds (300–450 kg)
DIET: Carnivore
KNOWN PREY: Smaller, plant-eating dinosaurs
FOSSILS FOUND: North America
LIVED: Early Jurassic

SPEED:	STRENGTH:	BRAINS:	ATTACK:	DEFENSE:
8	6	6	6	5

THE RIPPER

Dilophosaurus was large but light for its size. Its bones were long and slender. Its teeth were long and thin, too, but probably not strong enough to bite and kill prey. Scientists think it used its clawed feet and hands to rip prey apart.

THE SHOWDOWN

Two classic prehistoric animals face off. Will Eusmilus be able to get in position to deliver a killing bite? Or will Dilophosaurus take Eusmilus out with its clawed feet?

HEIGHT: 2.6 feet (0.8 m)
WEIGHT: Up to 400 pounds (200 kg)
DIET: Carnivore
KNOWN PREY: Smaller mammals
FOSSILS FOUND: North America, Europe, Asia
LIVED: Pleistocene

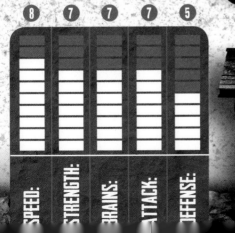

SPEED:	STRENGTH:	BRAINS:	ATTACK:	DEFENSE:
8	7	7	7	5

THE BITER

Eusmilus was a dangerous predator, with powerful legs and shoulders that helped it deliver a terrific downward thrust with its huge saber teeth. Prey didn't last long around this beast.

WINGSPAN: Up to 36 feet (11 m)
WEIGHT: 220 pounds (100 kg)
DIET: Carnivore
KNOWN PREY: Small dinosaurs, carrion
FOSSILS FOUND: North America
LIVED: Late Cretaceous

SPEED:	STRENGTH:	BRAINS:	ATTACK:	DEFENSE:
8	7	5	8	4

QUEEN OF THE SKY

This enormous creature soared on wind currents searching for prey. Its front limbs also had fingers that allowed it to walk on all fours when it was on the ground. Quetzalcoatlus nabbed its food with its sharp-edged beak.

THE SHOWDOWN

Two giant winged creatures fight it out mid-flight. Both have tremendous wingspans and sharp beaks. It may come down to who can stay aloft longer while dealing with punishing blows from talons and beaks. If they have to land, the Quetzalcoatlus will be able to walk on all fours, but the Ancient Giant Condor may be quick enough to stay out of its way.

SIZING THEM UP!

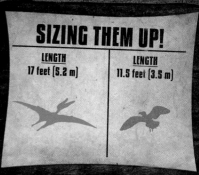

LENGTH	LENGTH
17 feet (5.2 m)	11.5 feet (3.5 m)

WINGSPAN: Up to 26 feet (8 m)
WEIGHT: 140–180 pounds (60–80 kg)
DIET: Carnivore
KNOWN PREY: Small mammals, carrion
FOSSILS FOUND: South America
LIVED: Late Miocene

8 5 6 6 2

SPEED: STRENGTH: BRAINS: ATTACK: DEFENSE:

POWERFUL FLIER

This massive, condor-like bird soared on thermal currents. When it spotted its prey, the Ancient Giant Condor was probably able to swoop down, grab, kill, and swallow it without even landing.

THERIZINOSAURUS VS. GIANT MONITOR LIZARD
(Megalania)

HEIGHT TO SHOULDER: 11–15 feet (3.3–4.5 m)
WEIGHT: Up to 5 tons
DIET: Herbivore or insectivore
NO KNOWN PREDATORS OR PREY
FOSSILS FOUND: Asia
LIVED: Late Cretaceous

"SCYTHE" LIZARD

Some paleontologists think the Therizinosaurus used its terrifying claws, which grew up to 30 inches (76 cm) long, to rip open termite nests and to tear bark off trees. Even so, they could also be used as defense against predators.

SPEED:	STRENGTH:	BRAINS:	ATTACK:	DEFENSE:
5	5	3	4	7

THE SHOWDOWN

This battle pits crazy claws against a monster of a lizard. Therizinosaurus's claws look dangerous, but if the Megalania gets its teeth on this odd dinosaur, its venomous bite will surely mean the end.

HEIGHT: 3.3 feet (1 m)
WEIGHT: Up to 1,268 pounds (575 kg)
DIET: Carnivore
KNOWN PREY: Large Australian megafauna
FOSSILS FOUND: Eastern Australia
LIVED: Pleistocene

3   7   2   9   9

SPEED: STRENGTH: BRAINS: ATTACK: DEFENSE:

THE MONSTER MONITOR

Like its modern cousin, the Komodo dragon, this enormous lizard may have had venomous spit that could have poisoned prey even after it took a bite. This large-mouthed predator also had scales like chain mail. It probably used its powerful tail to knock down prey.

DACENTRURUS VS. MARSUPIAL LION
(Thylacoleo carnifex)

HEIGHT TO SHOULDER: 4.9 feet (1.5 m)
WEIGHT: 2 tons
DIET: Herbivore
KNOWN PREDATOR: Allosaurus
FOSSILS FOUND: United Kingdom, Europe
LIVED: Late Jurassic

SPIKE

Dacentrurus was a type of stegosaur. It had pairs of triangular spike-like plates running down its back, ending in a spiked tail. For protection, it lowered its head and shoulders and swung its tail from side to side.

4	8	2	3	8
SPEED:	STRENGTH:	BRAINS:	ATTACK:	DEFENSE:

THE SHOWDOWN

This matchup puts a powerful defense against a strong offense. Will the Marsupial Lion be quick enough to get around the Dacentrurus's spiked plates and tail? If so, it can use its sharp teeth and claws to shred the big dinosaur.

SIZING THEM UP!

LENGTH	LENGTH
16 feet (4.9 m) or more	3.9 feet (1.2 m)

HEIGHT: 30 inches (75 cm)
WEIGHT: Up to 353 pounds (160 kg)
DIET: Carnivore
KNOWN PREY: Diprotodon
FOSSILS FOUND: Australia
LIVED: Pleistocene

7	6	6	8	4
SPEED:	STRENGTH:	BRAINS:	ATTACK:	DEFENSE:

CHEEKY LION

The largest Australian carnivore, the Marsupial Lion also had the strongest bite force of any mammalian predator. It had large "cheek" teeth (molars) for slicing and incisors for stabbing, and a retractable claw on each of its forelimbs for disemboweling prey.

LIOPLEURODON VS. MEGALODON

LENGTH: 82 feet (25 m)
WEIGHT: 75–150 tons
DIET: Carnivore
KNOWN PREY: Marine crocodiles, ichthyosaurs
FOSSILS FOUND: Europe, Asia
LIVED: Mid- to late Jurassic

SEA MONSTER

Liopleurodon holds the title for biggest carnivore that ever existed—and it was built to hunt. This monster was a powerful swimmer. Its 9.8-foot-long (3 m) mouth held rows of knife-like teeth that grew up to 8 inches (30 cm)—twice as long as T. rex's teeth.

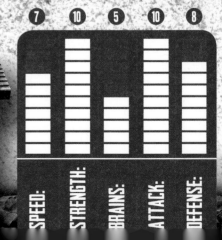

7	10	5	10	8
SPEED:	STRENGTH:	BRAINS:	ATTACK:	DEFENSE:

THE SHOWDOWN

Two giants of the deep go fin to fin—or tooth to tooth. Both are powerful swimmers and both have impressive mouthfuls of teeth. Liopleurodon is bigger, but not by much. And Megalodon weighs almost as much. Plus, Megalodon is known for the amazing strength of its bite.

SIZING THEM UP!

LENGTH 82 feet (25 m)	LENGTH 50 feet (16 m)

LENGTH: 50 feet (16 m)
WEIGHT: 70–100 tons
DIET: Carnivore
KNOWN PREY: Whales
FOSSILS FOUND: On all continents but Antarctica
LIVED: Middle Miocene

8 9 6 8 7

SPEED: STRENGTH: BRAINS: ATTACK: DEFENSE:

MEGATOOTH

Imagine an oversized great white shark with a mouthful of teeth over 7 inches long (18 cm). Scientists have found that Megalodon could bite with a force of up to 18.2 tons—compared to that, a great white's bite force of 1.8 tons seems wimpy.

DEINOSUCHUS VS. SMILODON

HEIGHT AT SHOULDER: 3.9 feet (1.2 m)
WEIGHT: 2–3 tons
DIET: Carnivore
KNOWN PREY: Large dinosaurs, sea turtles
FOSSILS FOUND: North America
LIVED: Late Cretaceous

5	10	5	10	8
SPEED:	STRENGTH:	BRAINS:	ATTACK:	DEFENSE:

TERRIBLE CROCODILE

With teeth able to crunch bone, Deinosuchus was able to take down even armored dinosaurs. Like modern-day crocs, it probably snapped into dinosaurs who came to the river to drink, then dragged them into the water, drowning them before finishing the meal.

THE SHOWDOWN

A classic battle at the watering hole: the crocodile-like dinosaur and the tiger-like beast. Deinosuchus's powerful jaws could easily disable Smilodon. But Smilodon could pierce the croc's head with its spear-like teeth.

SIZING THEM UP!

LENGTH 33 feet (10 m)	LENGTH Up to 8.2 feet (2.5 m)

HEIGHT AT SHOULDER: 3.9 feet (1.2 m)
WEIGHT: 440–710 pounds (200–320 kg)
DIET: Carnivore
KNOWN PREY: Large herbivores, such as bison and camel
FOSSILS FOUND: North America, Central America, South America
LIVED: Pleistocene

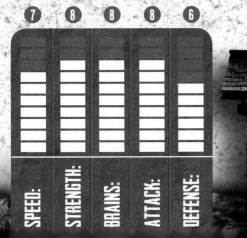

SPEED:	STRENGTH:	BRAINS:	ATTACK:	DEFENSE:
7	8	8	8	6

KNIFE TOOTH

Smilodon is often called a saber-toothed tiger or cat. It's most distinctive feature was its two huge canine teeth, each 7 inches (18 cm) long. It could open its jaws to an enormous 120 degrees—nearly completely open. Compare that to a cat's jaw, which open to 65 degrees.

CERATOSAURUS VS. EUROPEAN CAVE LION
(Panthera leo spelaea)

HEIGHT TO SHOULDER: 5 feet (1.5 m)
WEIGHT: Up to 1 ton
DIET: Carnivore
KNOWN PREY: Stegosaurs and sauropods
FOSSILS FOUND: North America, Africa
LIVED: Late Jurassic

HORNED LIZARD

Known by the horn on its snout, Ceratosaurus had strong legs, a massive body, and powerful jaws lined with sharp teeth. It may have hunted in packs and is thought to have high intelligence compared to other dinosaurs its size, making this one tricky dino to beat.

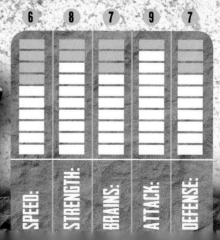

6	8	7	9	7
SPEED:	STRENGTH:	BRAINS:	ATTACK:	DEFENSE:

THE SHOWDOWN

Ceratosaurus is big, but the European Cave Lion is heavy and a skilled hunter. It can use powerful swipes of its paws and strong jaws to take down the dinosaur. But that's only if the Cave Lion can avoid Ceratosaurus's sharp teeth.

SIZING THEM UP!

LENGTH	LENGTH
20 feet (6 m)	Up to 11.5 feet (3.5 m)

HEIGHT: 4.3 feet (1.3 m)
WEIGHT: Up to 800 pounds (363 kg)
DIET: Carnivore
KNOWN PREY: Cave Bear
FOSSILS FOUND: Across Europe and Asia
LIVED: Pleistocene

7 7 8 7 4

SPEED: STRENGTH: BRAINS: ATTACK: DEFENSE:

POWERFUL PACK ANIMAL

Cave Lions are depicted in cave paintings, showing they had stripes like tigers and that they hunted in packs like modern lions. But a pack of Cave Lions would have been much more powerful, because a Cave Lion was 25 percent bigger than the biggest African lion on record today.

HYLAEOSAURUS VS. CAVE HYENA
(Crocuta spelaea)

HEIGHT TO SHOULDER: 6 feet (1.8 m)
WEIGHT: 2 tons
DIET: Herbivore
UNKNOWN PREDATORS AND PREY
FOSSILS FOUND: England
LIVED: Early Cretaceous

3 5 2 3 7

SPEED: STRENGTH: BRAINS: ATTACK: DEFENSE:

GENTLE GIANT
Hylaeosaurus was a plant-eating dinosaur. Though its belly was soft and easy
to pierce, its top and sides were entirely blanketed in heavy armored plates.
A predator would have to flip it over to wound it.

THE SHOWDOWN

Hylaeosaurus is enormous and covered with protective plates. But if the Cave Hyena is able to find its weak spot—its soft underbelly—it might have a chance at winning this matchup. Plus, the Hyena has the advantage of smarts. Its larger brain could give it the upper hand.

HEIGHT: 3.3 feet (1 m)
WEIGHT: 496 pounds (225 kg)
DIET: Carnivore, scavenger
KNOWN PREY: Woolly Rhinoceros, Cave Bear
FOSSILS FOUND: Africa
LIVED: Pleistocene

⑦ ⑤ ⑦ ⑦ ③

SPEED: STRENGTH: BRAINS: ATTACK: DEFENSE:

FIERCE HUNTER

Closely related to today's spotted hyena, the Cave Hyena was one of the top predators of its time. Despite its fierce nature, however, this beast probably took advantage of other predators by stealing their kill, too.

MASSOSPONDYLUS VS. ENTELODON

HEIGHT TO HIPS: 3 feet (1 m)
WEIGHT: 775 pounds (350 kg)
DIET: Herbivore
KNOWN PREDATOR: Dracovenator
FOSSILS FOUND: Africa, North America
LIVED: Early Jurassic

LONG NECKED

Massospondylus had a long neck, a very long tail, and a small head. It had five fingers on each hand, which it may have used for grasping. It was a fairly speedy sprinter and may have been able to run on two legs.

	6	5	1	4	4
	SPEED:	STRENGTH:	BRAINS:	ATTACK:	DEFENSE: